The Murder
At Emerson's

RUBY JANE SCHWIEGER

PUBLISHED BY

MINNETONKA, MN 55305
WWW.SIGMASBOOKSHELF.COM

The Murder at Emerson's by Ruby Jane Schwieger

Copyright © 2017 by Sigma's Book Shelf.

Printed in the United States of America

First Printing 2017

ISBN 978-0-9987157-0-4

Chapter One

This started out as a normal school year. I packed my bags, said goodbye to my mom, dad, dog, and beautiful Minnesota. As I walked on to the plane that would take me to my eighth grade year at Emerson's Boarding School, I had no idea that this year would be any different than the last.

I finally found my seat and waited for Calvin, who is one of my two best friends. He is a shy, yet super nice kid. Neena, my other best friend, is loud, a drama queen, outgoing, and will stand up for what she believes in (sometimes this does not sit well with our teachers). It is a miracle that Neena and Calvin get along; but we are three peas in a pod. It is nice to have friends you can trust.

Out of the corner of my eye, I saw Calvin hugging his mom goodbye (he is already taller than she is). As he entered the plane, he looked around for a second, and then saw me and waved.

"Calvin!" I exclaimed as I stood up and hugged him. "It has been so long!"

"I know," he replied as he stored his bag in the overhead. "It is good to see you."

"Ready for the four-hour flight to Washington?"

"Ready as I'll ever be."

Calvin is very scared of planes, especially taking off. He started shivering in fear.

"Calvin," I tried to comfort him, "take deep breaths. It's

okay." I put my arm around his shoulder. "How about watching a movie?" I asked as I pointed to the screen in front of him. "I heard most of them are free." He began sifting through films, and finally selected an old Western and plugged his headphones in.

The engines on the plane were revving up and we were beginning to roll down the runway. The look on Calvin's face showed pure fear. I smiled at him encouragingly. He nervously smiled back.

Three bags of chips, two movies, and one playlist later, we landed. Calvin looked so relieved.

"You know," he told me, "I love Emerson's, but the plane ride here sucks!"

We picked up all of our things, put them in our bags, and exited the plane. We were planning to meet Neena and her family at Gate 3. A quick look at the airport map showed that it was going to take a while to get there.

"It looks like we are going to need to take Monorail C. That would be the fastest way," Calvin said as he pointed to the map. "Plus," he added, "we can get off at Stop 2 and go to the food court."

"Yes! I am starving." We made our way to the monorail station and got on. It was packed with people and luggage, and we had to stand as we made our way back to the main terminal.

"Calvin," I said, "we need to get off here." We muscled our way through the crowd and barely got off before the doors shut behind us.

"Ahhh," Calvin said as he pointed to the food court, "the Holy Grail."

"Come on!" I laughed.

"What do you want?" I asked Calvin said as we walked into the food court.

"How about some Chinese food?"

"Okay." We walked to the Panda Express and each ordered chow mein to go.

We ate our food as we walked to Gate 3 to meet Neena and her family. When we finally got there, we started to look around for them. "See anything?" Calvin asked me.

"Nope," I replied."Maybe they-" Neena then slammed into me and Calvin and gave us a big bear hug.

"OMG YOU GUYS!!!" Neena shouted in delight. "I haven't seen you in forever!"

"Hi Neena," squeaked Calvin inside Neena's powerful hug. Neena has beautiful long black hair and is super short, so Calvin looked like a giant standing next to her.

"Hate to cut this short," Neena's mom said, "but you guys need to get to the van." Every year, an Emerson's van comes to pick up the students who arrive at the airport.

"Here you go," said Neena's dad as he wheeled over a luggage cart. He began to put all of our suitcases on the cart.

"Hurry up, Phil," said Neena's mom, "the kids can't miss the van."

"Okay, okay," he said. We started to hurry towards the parking lot. When we got there, it was pouring rain. We all ran to the van and Neena's dad shoved the luggage into the back as quickly as he could. Neena said hurried goodbyes to her parents and then joined us in the van.

"Wow!" Neena exclaimed while wringing her hair out. "Sure is raining!"

"Yeah it is," I replied. "I'm soaked!" There were a few other kids in the van with us. Two seventh graders on their phones and one high schooler eating some chips. "Uhh," Calvin groaned as he slumped down in his seat. "Now we get a two-hour drive to school."

As we started the rainy, gray drive to Emerson's Boarding School, I plugged my headphones in and fell asleep. It had been a long day of travel.

Chapter Two

Neena was the one who shook me awake. "Up, up, up!" she said. "We're here!" I sat up and looked out the window. When I first saw the campus every year, it took my breath away. It looked almost like a medieval castle, with gray stone buildings and gargoyles dotting them. The fall colors had not yet spread to the trees surrounding the campus, so it looked like it was in a misty green forest.

"Everybody over here!" yelled Mrs. Tomas, our English teacher. The students who had just gotten off the three vans came over. "Here are your student packets. They will tell you what dorm room you have and who you will share it with. The packets also include your class schedule. Dinner will be held in an hour, and we will give more information then." She handed out the packets and then went to inform the next group of students coming in.

"OMG EVA! We're sharing a room!" screamed Neena. "Thank the heavens!" I replied.

"Oh dang," Calvin muttered. "I'm with Dan." Dan was not necessarily a bully, but he could be annoying to be around.

"Sorry," Neena said with a hug.

"Well," Calvin said, "I guess we should go get our bags." We walked over to the van and the driver handed us our bags. "Well," Calvin said, "see you guys later." He walked away, studying the map to try and find his room.

"C'mon Eva!" said Neena as she walked into the main

building. Our student packets stated that our room was in the east wing, on the fourth floor. We dragged our suitcases up the stairs and finally found our room.

Neena opened the door, and what was inside was pretty normal. Two beds, two dressers, a lamp on each dresser, a desk and swivel chair, and a bookshelf.

"Time to decorate!" Neena squealed. Moving in was Neena's favorite part of each year. She got out her phone and turned on her playlist. She then proceeded to take out way more stuff than I thought was possible to cram into a suitcase.

I started to take out my clothes, fold them, and put them in my dresser. Neena took out (not kidding) a string of white Christmas lights and strung them over the bookshelf. Next, she took out a ton of books and some photos and organized the bookshelf. She went through the room and decorated every inch of it. It took about forty-five minutes.

When we were done, we stood back to admire (mostly Neena's) handiwork. "This looks great! I could admire this all day, but I am too hungry," I said.

"Same here," Neena replied, "and it's just about time for dinner!" We walked down the stairs to the mess hall. We searched the hallway for Calvin.

"Hey guys!" Calvin called out from behind us.

"AHHH!" Neena shrieked. "You almost scared me to death!" As Neena and Calvin were bickering, we entered the mess hall. No teachers were there.

"Um, you guys?" I interrupted my friends' arguing. "Where are the teachers?" There were plenty of students milling about, but no teachers.

"I hear somebody," Calvin said. "Over there." He pointed to the teachers' lounge, just down the hall. Sure enough, we could make out hushed voices. It sounded like they were arguing. We inched closer, and peeked into the door window. There were teachers in there. A lot of them.

We pressed our ears to the door. "I can't believe it! It just can't be!" said one of the voices.

"A student murdered! No, no, no! It's most likely a prank."

"It can't be," sobbed another voice. "The body was down the hall, and had a bloody knife in its side! I saw it!"

"Calm down. Calm down," said a masculine voice. "Has the area been sectioned off from all of the students?"

"Yes, but-"

"Well then, I think this can wait until after dinner."

"AFTER DINNER?" exclaimed a hysterical voice. "A STUDENT HAS JUST BEEN MURDERED! YOU EXPEC-"

"Quiet down!" said the male voice. "Do you want a student to hear this? We will talk after dinner."

The door started to open and we scattered down the hall. We looked back and saw the man coming out of the room eyeing us suspiciously. We walked towards the mess hall as Neena freaked out.

"OH. MY. GOD. EVA! CALVIN! SOMEONE GOT MURDERED! I THOUGHT THIS ONLY HAPPENED ON TV!" She started to hyperventilate.

"You guys, is this some kind of demented prank?" Calvin asked with fear in his eyes.

"I have no idea," I said.

"WAIT," Neena said slowly, "if a student got murdered- A MURDERER IS ON THE LOOSE! WE'RE ALL GONNA DIE!" She then proceeded to let out an extremely loud scream and fall on me.

"Neena!" I hissed. "Quit it!"

"Is she okay?" asked Janet, a girl in our grade.

"She will be fine," I said, "once she stops being a drama queen!" With that I shoved her off me. "C'mon," I said, "let's go to dinner."

At dinner, the announcements were totally regular. No mention of a murder whatsoever. The only weird thing the teachers said was not to go down the north wing of the second-floor hallway for any reason.

There was something fishy happening here. Something that I knew deep down I would have to unravel myself, and if I failed, my friends and I would be in very grave danger.

Chapter Three

After dinner, Neena was pacing around our room while I sat on my bed eating chips. "What do we do?" Neena asked me.

I thought about it for a minute. "We should investigate," I replied. "Obviously, the teachers are hiding something from us. We need to find out what it is."

"Are you crazy! We are going to get murdered too!"

"Fine. If you don't want to come, you don't have to, but I am going to investigate."

Neena looked at me. "Where are you going exactly?"

"To the north wing. The second-floor hallway."

"Oh great," Neena grumbled as she put on some shoes and walked out the door with me.

It was past 8:30, which meant that we weren't supposed to come out of our rooms. We had to be careful not to get caught. Also, we couldn't go get Calvin because we were not allowed in the boys' dormitories.

As we snuck through the deadly quiet, pitch black halls, our footsteps seemed to echo. The shadows on the wall warped into dark figures. It was terrifying.

"Eva," Neena whispered, "um, can we be done investigating now? Please? I do not want to see a body."

"We have to investigate," I whispered back, "and there probably won't be a body."

"Probably won't be? I could be up in my safe bed right now."

"Well, you can chicken out if you want."

That shut Neena up. We crept past the mess hall, the classrooms, and the gym before reaching the north wing.

"Ready?" I asked Neena.

"Ready," she replied.

We slowly walked up the stairs to get to the second floor. When we arrived, there was an area marked off with yellow tape, but nothing else. We suddenly saw two figures at the end of the hallway coming towards us. Neena and I dove into a classroom with the door propped open.

"Who was it?" said one of the voices. It sounded like our English teacher, Mrs. Tomas.

"That's the funny thing," said a man's voice, "the student who got murdered was not a student at all. We did a head count and everyone is accounted for, teachers and students."

"What?" Mrs. Tomas asked. "There is no way that could have happened. There should not be anyone on campus who isn't a student or teacher."

"Well, it did happen," said the man's voice, "and we are not going to call the police."

"Are you insane? We need to call the police! A kid got murdered! If we don't call the police who is going to get rid of the body?"

"There's another funny thing. We don't know where the body went. We thi-"

"YOU LOST THE BODY? HOW CAN YOU LOSE A BODY?"

"Calm down. What happened was Amy came to me in tears because she saw a body. I came up here and I saw it. I went for help and then it was gone. Just disappeared. And if we call the police we have NO evidence. They might even shut the school down. We can't let that happen now, can we?"

"HOW CAN YOU L-"

"Be quiet! Do you want somebody to hear us? No one knows the person who was murdered. No one. We have no evidence, no body. If we tell the cops, it will be for nothing and this school will get shut down."

"I will talk to you later about this."

Mrs. Tomas slowly walked over towards where we were hidden. As I looked to Neena in a panic, I realized we were hiding in her room.

She thankfully walked past us. When we thought the coast was clear, we came out of our hiding spot. As we walked down the stairs in stunned silence, we spotted Mrs. Tomas at the same time she spotted us.

"Why are you girls out of bed?" she asked sharply. "And why were you in the second-floor corridor, exactly where you shouldn't be?"

"Well," Neena said with newfound confidence, "Eva and I were up there because I needed a drink and the water tastes disgusting everywhere else. Don't worry, we used the buddy system because of the murder."

Mrs. Tomas frowned at us sternly then said, "Where did you get the idea that someone has been murdered at Emerson's? That's nonsense! Now go back to your room, and tomorrow after school, report to my room for detention."

"But-" Neena protested.

"My room, after school until 6 o clock for the next, hmm... 4 days."

"Uhhhhh," Neena groaned.

You couldn't get anything past Mrs. Tomas.

She escorted us back to our room without talking and shut the door firmly behind us.

"Wow," I said, stunned. "Now we really have to investigate. If the teachers won't call the cops, we could get murdered too."

"I think I have one lead," Neena said.

The room was silent for a second.

"Really? Well, are you going to tell me?"

"I think I should wait until tomorrow so I can tell Calvin too."

Neena smiled, knowing that this was going to drive me crazy.

"Fine," I huffed, and then got in my bed.

Chapter Four

My alarm rang at 6:00 a.m. I jumped out of bed and started to get ready for the school day. Neena, however, groaned and stuck her head under her pillow.

"Five more minutes…" she mumbled.

"Nope," I said. "I will not be late for breakfast again because of you."

With that I dragged her off her bed.

"Let go of me!" Neena yelled as she jumped up.

"Well, at least you're up now," I said cheerfully as I gathered up all of the notebooks and binders I needed for the day.

After Neena's long morning routine, we finally headed down to breakfast and grabbed our trays. We got in line for pancakes and saw Calvin walking towards us.

"Hi guys," he said.

"We have something important to tell you," I whispered.

Neena and I proceeded to hastily tell him about our investigation.

"Wow," he said, "that is a lot of good information. I am assuming that we are investigating further?"

"Yup," I answered, "and I think Neena has a great lead."

Calvin and I looked at Neena curiously.

"So," Neena started to explain her theory, "when Mrs. Tomas and that man were talking, they said the body was not one of the students. They also said it was a boy. I know for a fact that one of the groundskeepers, Greg, has a son who lives on the campus and is homeschooled."

We sat down and started to eat our pancakes and eggs.

"Wait," Calvin asked with a full mouth, "groundskeepers live 'ere?"

"Um, yeah," Neena replied, "ever wonder what the cottages behind the north wing are for? Anyway, Greg homeschools his son, so the son lives here with him."

"So," Calvin asked and then swallowed, "are you saying that you think Greg's son was murdered?"

"Exactly," Neena replied.

"Wait, wait, wait," I said. "Neena, how do you know all of this?"

Neena had never given school a second thought as long as I have known her. I was surprised that she even knew that the school employed groundskeepers, let alone what one's name was and that he homeschooled his son.

"Oh," Neena brushed off my question, "my parents know him. Anyway, when should we investigate?"

"During dinner. Nobody will miss us," I replied.

It was true. Dinner was super loud and crowded and the teachers did not take attendance.

"See ya then," Neena said, waltzing away with her empty tray.

Chapter Five

After struggling through science, math, art, choir and French, it was finally time for dinner. Neena, Calvin, and I met up by the mess hall.

"Can we please get something to eat first?" Calvin begged.

"No," Neena said firmly.

"C'mon Neena," I said, "we know you are hungry too." I made a begging face.

A small smile spread across her face. "Fine," she agreed.

We grabbed a bag of chips each and made for the exit.

"Which house is Greg's?" Calvin asked.

"I don't know," Neena said. "We just have to find out."

We walked out to the groundskeeper's houses and knocked on one of the doors. A man with a beard and overalls came out.

"Hello," he said cheerfully.

"Excuse me," I asked, "are you Greg?"

"Nope," he replied. "My name is Robert. Greg lives in the house over there." He pointed to a house about 20 feet away.

"Thanks," I said.

"No problem."

We walked over to the house Robert pointed at.

"Ready?" Neena asked us.

"No," Calvin said nervously.

Neena knocked on Greg's door.

There was a moment of silence. We looked at each other.

"I'm having second thoughts," Neena said. "We should just leave."

The door suddenly opened.

An angry man dressed in jeans and a plaid shirt looked at us.

"What the hell are you doin' out here? Students are eatin' dinner right now," Greg said while glaring at us.

Calvin looked like he was about to faint.

"Well, sir," I said timidly, "um, my friend here, Neena, had something to ask you."

If looks could kill, Neena would have murdered me.

"Um," Neena said super quickly, "there was a murder at school and I thought your son might have been the one murdered. But that is silly, so we are just going to leave your property before you shoot us because I strongly suspect you have a shotgun somewhere in there."

"Damn right I do," Greg said, "and you shouldn't be pokin' your nose in stuff that doesn't concern you!"

With that, he slammed the door in our faces.

"Well, isn't he a little ray of sunshine," I said.

"Yeah," Calvin said shakily.

"I'm sorry, you guys," Neena apologized. "I shouldn't have dragged you down here. I was just so excited. I really thought I had a lead."

"It's okay," I said. "I got us in trouble with Mrs. Tomas. WAIT! Mrs. Tomas! Detention! Neena, we have to go!"

"Sorry, Calvin!" Neena yelled over her shoulder.

Neena and I sprinted as fast as we possibly could back to school. The wind whipped our hair over our shoulders and stung our faces. The ground seemed to blur beneath our feet. When we reached the door, Neena flung it open with a giant bang. We ran up the stairs and burst into Mrs. Tomas's room.

"We're here!" Neena yelled.

Silence.

Mrs. Tomas was not in her room.

"Um," Neena said slowly as she looked around, "Mrs. Tomas?"

"What time is it?" I asked Neena in a panic, thinking that we might have missed detention.

She looked at her watch. "4:15. Dinner only ended 15 minutes ago. I say we should go back to our room. This is getting creepy."

"Okay," I said halfheartedly. I thought something fishy was happening here. Why would Mrs. Tomas not be there? She never misses detentions. Never.

Chapter Six

"I think we should stop investigating," Neena said as we walked back to our room. "That Greg guy was right. We shouldn't poke our nose in stuff that's not our business. I don't want to get involved in anything dangerous."

"Well," I replied, "it's going to be more dangerous if we don't investigate. Did you hear that man talking to Mrs. Tomas? They are not going to call the police."

"Then we can call the police!"

"There is no evidence. We need evidence."

"No we don't! Eva, you are not a detective. I don't want you to get hurt! We call the police, and they deal with this. It is not reasonable to put a MURDER on the back of an eighth grader!"

"But if we don't find the murderer and prove that he has nothing to do with the school, Emerson's will get shut down! This is an amazing school, Neena! If we stay on the paths we are on, we could get into a great college! Ivy League, even! Don't you see?"

"The police can solve this!"

"The police have NO EVIDENCE! NO EVIDENCE, NEENA! WE HAVE TO DO THIS OURSELVES!"

"Please don't do this, Eva. Please! I am begging you!"

"NO! I don't care what you say Neena. I will investigate this!"

"Fine. Don't say I didn't warn you."

A sack was then shoved over my head from behind.

I tried to struggle away, but the hands around my neck grasped me tightly.

"Quick!" Neena hissed. "We have to get her in the van before anyone sees us!"

"On it," a man's voice says.

"I've got the other one," a voice crackles through a walkie talkie.

I know I should have been paralyzed with fear, but I wasn't. The only emotion I had at that moment was pure rage.

"I TRUSTED YOU!" I yelled at Neena.

Neena, my friend. Neena, the traitor.

Chapter Seven

I was forced into what I thought was the back of a van. The rough cotton sack on my head scratched my face. My shins throbbed where I smacked them while being shoved into the van. My hands were bound behind my back.

I also found out who 'the other one' was.

Calvin.

He was shoved in the van after me.

"Neena?" Calvin asked, obviously terrified, "Eva?"

"Neena is not here, Calvin." I replied sharply.

"Where is she?"

"In the front seat."

"What?"

"She gave us away to these guys. She let this happen! But why? WAIT! CALVIN! What if Neena is the murderer?"

"NO! She can't be! Neena would never kill somebody! "

"How do you know? Neena let people KIDNAP us!"

At this point me and Calvin painfully bonked heads because we couldn't see each other.

"Ow," Calvin yelped.

"What if Neena is the murderer?" I asked him quietly.

"Well, then she has problems."

"How could we have been best friends with a murderer?"

"Eva," Calvin said gently, "you are jumping to conclusions. You are thinking of the worst possible scenario."

"But-"

"Eva, stop. There is no point in worrying about it when we don't know."

We sat in the bouncing van for a few minutes without talking.

Then, the reality of what was happening came crashing down around me.

"CALVIN!"

"Huh?"

"We are being kidnapped!"

"I know."

"We need to come up with a plan on how to escape!"

"We can't see, we can't use our hands, and we are locked in a van. What do we do?"

"Well, they were stupid to put both of us in here because we can untie the ropes around each other's hands."

"We can?"

"I think so. Turn around and I will try to untie yours."

I fumbled with the ropes for a while, but eventually got them untied.

"Thanks!"

"Now untie the sack."

The sacks over our heads had a rope tied around our neck to keep them on.

"Got it," Calvin said, "now let me get your hands."

He untied the ropes around my wrists and took the sack off my head.

I looked around the interior of the van. It had paint chipping off the sides and rust on the floor. Other than me and Calvin, it was completely empty.

"What do we do now?" Calvin asked.

"I don't know," I replied. "Maybe we could just burst out when they open the doors. They don't expect us to be able to see and use our hands."

"I'm not sure it will work. Maybe we should follow orders."

"Calvin!" I hissed. "We might be getting there soon, wher-ever there is! We need to do my plan!"

"No!" Calvin hissed back. "Quick, get your ropes back on!"

"We have no idea what they will do!"

"Well, we should-"

At that moment, the van lurched to a stop.

"Your plan it is," Calvin whispered.

The doors slowly started to open.

Calvin and I burst out, shoving whoever the person open-ing the doors was aside. All around us was dark forest. There was one building, what looked like a farmhouse, straight ahead. We ran for it.

The cold wind slapped our faces and we heard muffled shouts behind us. We had no idea why we were running to this house, but we were. We didn't know if it was the bad guy's hideout or the house of some granny. The adrenaline surged through my body and the only thought I could think was: RUN!

We finally got to the door, which fortunately was unlocked and burst in.

Chapter Eight

The inside of the house was dark and quiet. Calvin and I quickly peeked out one of the windows to see if anyone was coming. One dark figure was running towards the house we were in.

"Hide!" I hissed at Calvin.

We ran into a nearby room, and hid behind a big, plush chair.

We heard the front door bang open.

"Eva!" A voice yelled. "Calvin! I know you are in here!"

Calvin and I looked at each other. The voice was Neena's.

"Please come out. Nobody else is here. I told them you ran into the woods, so they are looking for you there."

"How can we trust you?" I yelled back.

Neena zeroed in on my voice and started to walk to the room we were hidden in.

"You can't. I'm sorry, I let you guys down."

I wanted to yell back, but she was too close for comfort.

"Please just come out. I can explain everything! I promise!"

She walked into the room we were hiding in.

Calvin looked at me. I nodded. We stood up from behind the chair.

"Fine," I said, "start talking."

She looked at us for a moment.

"I should probably start from the beginning. This summer I got an e-mail from some random person asking if I went to Emerson's Boarding School. I replied and said I did. They wrote back asking me if I was interested in a job. I said yes. Okay, I realize now that it was not a good idea to interact with a stranger I met on the Internet, but just let me talk. After I sent them the e-mail, they wrote back that if I want this job, which they said would pay a lot, I could not tell my parents, my friends, anyone. They told me if I accepted this, I would be sworn into this community thing for the rest of my life. I asked them how much this job would pay, and they told me $5,000. That's a lot of money. I couldn't say no!"

"What was the job?" Calvin asked.

"It was for me to stage a murder scene inside Emerson's," Neena replied.

"But why would they want you to do this? Who was your employer?" I asked Neena.

"I think it was some crime organization. You know, they get a client that wants an illegal job done and they do it for lots of money," Neena answered, looking down in shame.

"And you knew this?" Calvin asked, outraged.

Neena burst into tears. "No! I was stupid enough to take the job. I figured it all out in the van, so I got scared for you guys and sent the kidnappers into the woods to look for you."

"Okay," I said slowly, "so, if you took a job from a crime organization, who was your original client? I mean, who originally wanted you to stage a murder scene?"

"Well," Neena said with a sniff, "I don't think that I am supposed to know this, but I overheard the guys in the van talking, and they mentioned something about a rival school. I would bet anything that rival school wanted Emerson's shut down so they would get more business."

"How did you do it?" Calvin asked Neena.

"Stage the murder? It was easy. The people I worked for sent me there a day early with this other kid, Brandon. All I had to do was take some of that fake blood and the fake knife that they gave me and make Brandon look like a corpse. I waited in the supply closet until some teachers saw the scene, then I helped Brandon make his getaway."

"Why did you scare the teachers?" Calvin asked.

"Actually, that wasn't supposed to happen," Neena replied. "The client wanted the students to see the body and call 911, which would get the school shut down. We had to take Brandon away because if people started poking around, they would discover he was a fake corpse and call the cops."

"That makes sense," I told Neena, "but WHY ON EARTH DID YOU KIDNAP US?"

Neena started to cry again.

"I thought I was done," she said in a quaking voice, "but they offered me another job. For another $5,000 dollars. The first job was so easy, so why should I not take the other one? I did, and it was to make sure nobody started investigating the "murder". You did, so I took you to Greg, and he is the meanest person on campus, so I thought it would persuade you to not investigate. It didn't and I let you guys get captured. I am the worst friend in the world!"

With that, she started to sob.

"I believe you so far, but who are the people that were in the van?" Calvin asked Neena.

"I'm not sure," she replied, still crying. "All I know is that they are employed by the same person I was."

"Neena, I trusted you and you let people kidnap us," I told her.

"I am so sorry! I don't deserve to have friends like you! I shouldn't have been tempted by all that money! I will understand if you guys give me up to the cops."

Calvin and I looked at each other.

"Should we?" I asked.

Calvin shook his head slightly. "She is our friend."

I agreed. Neena was our friend. She made up for her

mistakes by distracting our kidnappers, and I truly did trust her.

"No," I said, "we won't give you up to the cops."

Neena grabbed us into one of those giant bear hugs she is known for.

"I love you guys!" she yelled, and for the first time that day, I smiled.

"Now let's go kick some bad guy but!" Neena yelled. "Actually, no, we should call the cops."

Chapter Nine

After Neena called the cops, we sat around and stared out the window until we saw the red and blue lights and heard sirens. The police drove up, and thankfully the van was still there. All three of us rushed out to meet them.

"Where are they?" asked a policewoman.

"They ran into the woods," Neena told them.

"Thanks for the tip," said a policeman, "but once we get you guys back to your school, there will be more questioning."

"That is fine with me," Calvin said, obviously relived this fiasco was over.

"Actually," the policeman said, "we have had a lot of trouble for the past few months with some crime organization. Your comments could be pretty helpful."

"Really?" I asked.

"Don't even," said Calvin. "I know that look in your eye, Eva, and we are not getting ourselves almost killed again!"

Neena and I burst out laughing.

"Excuse me," Neena laughed, "I was the one in real danger here. I could have grown up to be Al Capone or something!"

"Yeah, and Eva and I could have been killed!"

As I watched them bicker, I knew Neena would be forgiven, and we would have good times again.

Epilogue

Emerson's Boarding School was not shut down because of the staged murder. In fact, even more students enrolled because of all the media coverage surrounding the plot.

Eva, Calvin, and Neena are still best friends. Calvin is also becoming friends with his "annoying" roommate Dan.

Neena had a court case where they decided her punishment for helping with the staged murder. The judge was lenient with her since she was obviously sorry for what she had done, and she gave helpful information to the cops. Her sentence was a 10-day suspension from Emerson's, a $100 fine, and enrollment in an Internet safety class.

The reason Mrs. Tomas wasn't in her room when Neena and Eva went in for detention was because she was making some copies in the copy room. She came back to her room a few minutes after they left and proceeded to write each of them up for missing detention. Their punishment, an extra day of detention.

The criminal organization that hired Neena has still not been caught, but Neena gave the police some helpful tips that were used to identify the kidnappers in the van. The police say they are more optimistic than ever with this case. Now they at least know the identities of a few of the people involved in the organization.

Greg's homeschooled son turned out to be Brandon, the "corpse" that Neena worked with. Greg was mean to them because he didn't want them to figure out the mystery and his son's role in it.

Brandon confessed to the police and was truly sorry for what he did. He said he thought he would just be playing a prank, not trying to shut the school down. He also got enrolled in an Internet safety class and had to pay a $100 dollar fine.

Neena and Brandon have become good friends, and Greg has decided to apply for a scholarship offered to the children of school employees so Brandon can go to Emerson's with his new friends - Neena, Eva, and Calvin.

Sigma's Bookshelf (www.SigmasBookshelf.com) is an independent book publishing company that exclusively publishes the work of teenage authors, who are between the ages of 12 - 19. The company was founded in 2016 by Minnesota teenager Justin M. Anderson, whose first book, "Saving Stripes: A Kitty's Story," was published when he was 14, and has since sold hundreds of copies.

"I know there are a lot of other teenagers out there who are good writers and deserve to have their work published, but don't have access to the kinds of resources I do," he said. So, with the help of his parents, Justin started up what is believed to be the first publishing company exclusively for teenage authors.

Sigma's Bookshelf is a sponsored project of Springboard for the Arts, a nonprofit arts service organization. Contributions on behalf of Sigma's Bookshelf may be made payable to Springboard for the Arts and are tax deductible to the extent permitted by law. Donations can be made online at www.SigmasBookshelf.com/donate.